To our super twins Thomas and Kate,
for teaching us the meaning of infinite love.
—SKE and KEH

To the "Patatale" illustrator kids who have
chosen me as their "Mom," because family is
sometimes a matter of ink.
—MR

🐝 little bee books

New York, NY
Text copyright © 2022 by Sarah Kate Ellis and Kristen Ellis-Henderson
Illustration copyright © 2022 by Max Rambaldi
All rights reserved, including the right of reproduction
in whole or in part in any form.
Manufactured in China RRD 1021
First Edition
2 4 6 8 10 9 7 5 3 1
Library of Congress Cataloging-in-Publication Data is available upon request.
ISBN 978-1-4998-1263-3
littlebeebooks.com
glaad.org
For information about special discounts on bulk purchases,
please contact Little Bee Books at sales@littlebeebooks.com.

A PROUD PARTNERSHIP BETWEEN
glaad + 🐝 little bee books
A portion of the proceeds from the sale of this
book will be donated to accelerating
LGBTQ acceptance.

All Moms

Sarah Kate Ellis and Kristen Ellis-Henderson
Illustrated by Max Rambaldi

little bee books

Some moms are silly.
Some play guitar.

Some moms fly airplanes and others fix cars.

Some moms make signs
and march in parades.

Some moms give kisses
and make lemonade.

But all moms
will help you
and come to
your aid.

Some moms are sporty.
Some craft and paint.

Some moms are early
and others are late.

Some moms are bosses
when they go to work.

Some moms are doctors and fix peoples hurts.

But all moms love birthdays and yummy desserts.

Sometimes, it's one mom who gets it all done.

They work twice as hard
to make our lives fun.

Janie's two dads give hugs
just like moms.

Joey

And Joey's great nana
sings lullaby songs.

But all are there
to help us get strong.

Some moms give snuggles.
Some play pretend.

Some moms read stories
or help you make friends.

Some moms encourage
when you're feeling shy.

Some moms hold you
whenever you cry.

But all moms' love
is as big as the sky.